Disney

ZOOTOPIA
CROCHET

KATI GÁLUSZ

D0896258

THUNDER BAY
P · R · E · S · S

Thunder Bay Press
An imprint of Printers Row Publishing Group
A division of Readerlink Distribution Services, LLC
10350 Barnes Canyon Road, Suite 100, San Diego, CA 92121
www.thunderbaybooks.com

Copyright © & TM 2017 Disney Enterprise, Inc.

All rights reserved. No part of this publication may be reproduced, distributed, or transmitted in any form or by any means, including photocopying, recording, or other electronic or mechanical methods, without the prior written permission of the publisher, except in the case of brief quotations embodied in critical reviews and certain other noncommercial uses permitted by copyright law.

Printers Row Publishing Group is a division of Readerlink Distribution Services, LLC.
Thunder Bay Press is a registered trademark of Readerlink Distribution Services, LLC.

All notations of errors or omissions should be addressed to Thunder Bay Press, Editorial Department, at the above address. All other correspondence (author inquiries, permissions) concerning the content of this book should be addressed to becker&mayer! Books, 11120 NE 33rd Place, Ste. 101, Bellevue, WA 98004.

This book is part of the *Disney Zootopia Crochet* kit and is not to be sold separately.

Produced by becker&mayer!,
a division of Quarto Publishing Group USA Inc.
Bellevue, WA

Designer: Sam Dawson
Editor: Dana Youlin
Photographer: Chris Burrows
Production coordinator: Olivia Holmes

Thunder Bay Press
Publisher: Peter Norton
Publishing Team: Lori Asbury, Ana Parker, Kathryn Chipinka, Aaron Guzman
Editorial Team: JoAnn Padgett, Melinda Allman, Traci Douglas
Production Team: Jonathan Lopes, Rusty von Dyl

Project #16533
ISBN-13: 978-1-68412-017-8

Printed, manufactured, and assembled in
Shenzhen, China.

21 20 19 18 17   1 2 3 4 5

MIX
Paper from
responsible sources
FSC® C017606
www.fsc.org

Contents

Introduction

Zootopia is a city like no other, with diverse climate zones ranging from arctic to tropical, and multi-scaled infrastructure to accommodate all citizens from the tiniest mice to the tallest giraffes. Yet it is familiar to all of us, from the gadgets these talking, well-dressed animals use and the slowness of bureaucracy to the way hate and prejudice can tear apart society. We can all recognize ourselves in its likeable but flawed protagonists, who make mistakes but keep trying to make their world a better place.

Whether you plan to crochet these figures as a play set for a child or a cheer-up gift for an older fan, they are guaranteed to induce many smiles. I hope you will have as much fun making them as I had designing them!

Happy crocheting,

Kati Gálusz

What's Included

This kit contains the tools and materials you will need to make one Judy and one Nick doll: yarn in gray, cream, pink, black, blue, orange, brown, beige, and green; embroidery floss in pink, black, yellow, purple, and indigo; two pairs of plastic safety eyes; a D/3 (3.25mm) crochet hook; a large needle; and stuffing.

Abbreviation Chart

BLO	back loop only
ch	chain or chains
dc	double crochet
FLO	front loop only
hdc	half-double crochet
inc	increase
invdec	invisible decrease
rnd	round
sc	single crochet
sl st	slip stitch
st	stitch or stitches
YO	yarn over

Notes on Tools and Materials

YARN

I prefer to use acrylic yarn for amigurumi (the Japanese word, now used worldwide, for knitted or crocheted stuffed figures) because it is easily available, comes in a wide range of colors, and works up into sturdy, machine-washable pieces.

The patterns in this book were designed with light worsted/DK yarn. But you could use any yarn thickness: as long as you use the same weight of yarn throughout, your dolls will turn out just fine—only smaller or bigger than the originals.

Changing yarn size between dolls is a great way to ramp up the size difference between figures: for example, Koslov made of super bulky yarn and Mr. Big made of fingering weight yarn would look very cool together!

You will need much less than a skein of each color, so these dolls are a perfect way to use up leftover yarn. However, it is best to stick to the same brand throughout a project, as different brands might work up differently even though they are officially the same thickness.

GAUGE AND HOOK SIZE

Exact gauge is not important in these projects as long as you work tightly enough to create a fabric that doesn't gap visibly when you stuff the toy. To achieve this, you will need a hook size smaller than recommended on the yarn's label. I prefer to use D/3 (3.25mm) for light worsted and E/4 (3.5mm) for worsted yarn, but these are only guidelines; feel free to experiment to find what best suits your yarn choice and crocheting style.

STITCH MARKERS

These are sometimes necessary to mark a certain stitch. And, as most amigurumi is worked in a continuous spiral without joining, you will also need a stitch marker to keep track of your rounds. There are special split-ring markers for crochet, but safety pins or paper clips work just as well.

STUFFING

I recommend polyester fiberfill, as it is easily available and economical, and makes resilient, washable toys. Stuffing settles over time, so (unless instructed otherwise) always stuff pieces firmly so they will look good for a long time. A pair of tweezers can come in handy when you need to stuff through small openings.

EMBROIDERY FLOSS

Embroidery floss is loosely twisted from six thin cotton strands. To crochet, use floss right as it comes from the skein. For embroidery, always start with separating the individual strands (even if you need to use all six); this will produce flatter, smoother stitches.

FELT

Some projects in this book include details made of felt. For bigger pieces on light colors, you can use an erasable marker to trace the template to the felt. On dark

colors or for tiny pieces, I prefer to stick the template to the felt with clear adhesive tape, then use small scissors to cut out the shape.

NEEDLES AND PINS

Blunt tapestry needles are usually recommended for sewing knit and crochet pieces, but for amigurumi I prefer a chenille needle (large embroidery needle) because its sharp point can pierce through yarn if necessary for a neat join.

For finer embroidered details like mouths, it might be easier if you use a sewing needle or small embroidery needle rather than a yarn-sized needle.

Craft pins are necessary to hold pieces together while you sew them.

GLUE

Some projects need glue for finishing. I recommend using fabric glue: it is easy to apply precisely, and it dries clear, so small mistakes will be practically invisible.

PLASTIC SAFETY EYES

The eye sizes in this book are applicable for light worsted yarn; if you use a different yarn thickness, you will need to adjust the eye size accordingly.

For perfectly placed eyes, stuff the head and use pins to find the right position. Stick the eyes in place, then remove the stuffing so you can attach the washers. Washers should be pushed onto the eye stems with the bulge pointing away from the eye.

Please note that even though safety eyes are highly unlikely to come off, small plastic parts should always be considered a choking hazard for babies. If making dolls for a young recipient, use embroidery to create the eyes (and omit other potentially dangerous items like beads and wires).

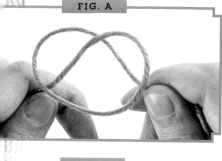

FIG. A

Crochet Stitches and Techniques

This chapter contains a short primer on the techniques you will need for amigurumi. If you are new to crochet, I suggest practicing the basics before attempting the projects in this book. Many yarn shops offer classes, or you can look up video tutorials online.

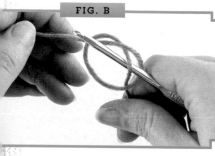

FIG. B

SLIPKNOT

Use this to begin a chain. Make a loop on your yarn a few inches from the end. Insert your hook through the loop and grab the yarn end connected to the skein. Pull the strand through the loop, then tighten the knot. **(FIGS. A & B)**

YARN OVER (YO)

Wrap the yarn around your hook from back to front.

CHAIN (CH)

Make a slipknot first (unless you are in the middle of a piece and already have a loop on your hook). YO and pull yarn through the loop on hook. Repeat as many times as required. **(FIG. C)**

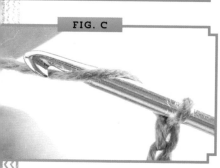

FIG. C

The loop on the hook doesn't count as a chain, so omit it if you are checking the stitch count.

WORKING INTO A CHAIN

Usually, you have to skip the ch nearest to the hook and work your first st in the second ch from hook. (The pattern will always specify this.)

When you look at a row of chains, the front side will look like a series of tiny Vs, and the back will have a single ridge of loops. **(FIG. D)** If you want your piece to look really neat, insert your hook into the back ridge rather than the front V. **(FIG. E)**

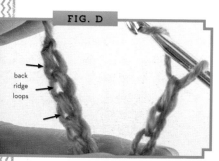

FIG. D

back ridge loops

WORKING INTO STITCHES

Every stitch has two strands in a small V shape on top. Insert your hook under both sides of the V unless otherwise specified.

WORKING IN FRONT/BACK LOOP ONLY (FLO/BLO)

When you look at the V on top of the stitch, the strand closest to you is called the front loop and the strand farthest from you is called the back loop. If you need to work in FLO, insert your hook under the closest loop only. If you need to work BLO, insert your hook under the farthest loop only.

SINGLE CROCHET (SC)

This is the stitch you will use most for amigurumi. Insert your hook into the st or ch, YO **(FIG. F)**, and draw up a loop (pull yarn through st or ch). You will have two loops on your hook. YO and pull yarn through both loops on hook. **(FIG. G)**

INCREASE (INC)

In these patterns, inc always means single-crochet increase: work two sc in the same st or ch.

INVISIBLE DECREASE (INVDEC)

While this stitch can be replaced by the more common *single-crochet-2-together* decrease, the invisible decrease (invdec) produces a much smoother look, so it's really worth learning for amigurumi.

Insert your hook in the front loop only of the st (no YO here!). Swing the hook slightly downward so you can insert it into the front loop of the next st. YO **(FIG. H)** and pull the yarn through both front loops. Then YO again and pull through the two loops on the hook.

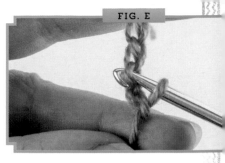

FIG. E

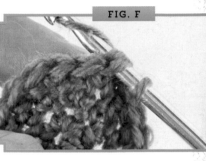

FIG. F

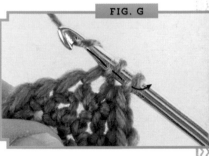

FIG. G

FIG. H

SLIP STITCH (SL ST)

Insert your hook into the st or ch, YO, and pull yarn through both the st or ch and the loop on hook. **(FIG. I)**

Be careful to keep the stitch loose: the V on top should be the same size as the top of other stitches. If your sl st is too tight, you won't be able to insert your hook in the next round, or your work might pucker.

HALF DOUBLE CROCHET (HDC)

YO, insert your hook into the st or ch, YO, and draw up a loop (creating three loops on the hook). YO and pull through all three loops on the hook. **(FIG. J)**

DOUBLE CROCHET (DC)

YO, insert your hook into the st or ch, YO, and draw up a loop (creating three loops on the hook). **(FIG. K)** YO and pull through two loops on the hook, then YO again and pull through the remaining two loops on the hook.

PUFF STITCH

*YO, insert your hook into the st, YO, and draw up a loop. Repeat from * twice, inserting your hook into the same st—you will end up with seven loops on your hook. YO and pull through all loops on the hook. **(FIG. L)**

SKIP STITCHES

Leave the required number of st unworked and continue in the next st, working in the same direction as before.

FASTEN OFF

To finish your piece, cut the yarn four to five inches from your hook (or more, if you will need the yarn end for sewing), and pull the end through the last loop on the hook.

CLOSE THE REMAINING HOLE

Insert your hook through the front loop of the next st and pull through the yarn end. Repeat in each st around the hole, then pull the end to close the gap. Thread the remaining end in a needle and push through the center, and the seam will become almost invisible.

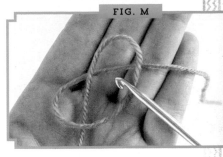

FIG. M

WEAVE IN YARN ENDS

In amigurumi, many yarn ends are luckily on the inside of the piece, so we don't have to deal with them. But there is a dangling end left after closing up a body part, as well as the leftover yarn after sewing together pieces. To secure these, stitch through the body several times to catch it in the stuffing. Then pull the yarn tight and cut it right in front of the crochet fabric—the tension will pull it back inside the body.

For flat pieces, you need to weave in the end by sewing through several stitches, then snip off the rest as close to the fabric as possible.

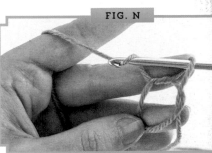

FIG. N

WORKING IN ROUNDS

Amigurumi is mostly crocheted in rounds, starting with a small circle of stitches and progressing in a continuous spiral without turning or joining. To keep track of the beginnings/ends of your rounds, attach a stitch marker in the first st of the round, moving it to the next round when you start it.

RIGHT SIDE

FIG. O

MAGIC RING

The magic ring is a nice technique to start working in the round, because it will create a small circle of stitches with no gap in the center.

Form a circle with the yarn and insert your hook through this ring **(FIG. M)**, YO and draw up a loop, then ch 1. **(FIG. N)**

WRONG SIDE

FIG. P

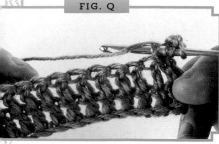

FIG. Q

FIG. R

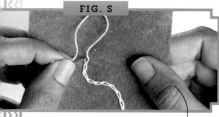

FIG. S

Work the first round of stitches over the two strands of yarn, then pull on the free end to close the ring.

RIGHT AND WRONG SIDE

If you are working in rounds, there will be a right and a wrong side: the right side is the side facing you while you work; this should be the outside of your piece. On the right side, individual stitches resemble small Vs. **(FIG. O—PAGE 11)** On the wrong side, they are like an upside down V with a horizontal bar on top. **(FIG. P—PAGE 11)**

It is quite usual for your work to start curling up in the wrong direction. Stop after the first two or three rounds to check, and if necessary turn the piece right side out.

WORKING IN ROWS

Working in rows means turning your piece at the end of every row and working in the opposite direction in the next row. To allow for this, you will have to crochet one or more "turning chain(s)" at the end of the row. **(FIG. Q)**

Turning chains don't count as regular stitches, so omit them if you are checking your stitch count.

CHANGE COLORS

When you are crocheting the last st with the old color, stop when you have the last two loops on the hook. **(FIG. R)** YO with the new color and pull it through the loops on the hook. Cut the old color, and tie the two ends together on the inside.

Embroidery Stitches

CHAIN STITCH

The chain stitch looks like it could be

part of the crochet fabric, so it is a good choice to add details to amigurumi.

Bring up the needle at the starting point. Insert it again at the same place and bring it out a stitch length ahead. Pass the needle through the loop and tighten the stitch. Try to keep each chain the same size. **(FIG. S)**

BACK STITCH

This stitch is perfect for fine lines, whether they should be straight or follow complicated designs.

Start by making a simple straight stitch. For each subsequent stitch, bring the needle out one stitch length ahead, and down again at the end of the previous stitch. **(FIG. T)**

Construction Technique Used in All Patterns

All projects in this book share a construction method: the legs are made first from the feet up, then joined to continue with the torso.

Put the legs together with the feet pointing forward and out. Find the two innermost stitches that are touching, insert your hook through these stitches **(FIG. U)**, and pull through the specified yarn. Tie a double knot to fix the legs together. Again insert your hook into the same stitches and draw up a loop, then ch 1. **(FIG. V)**

To crochet the first round of the body, turn the piece so that the feet are looking away from you and start to crochet, first on the left leg going around from rear to front **(FIG. W)**, then continue around the right leg. Work a sc in each stitch except the two that were used to tie the legs together.

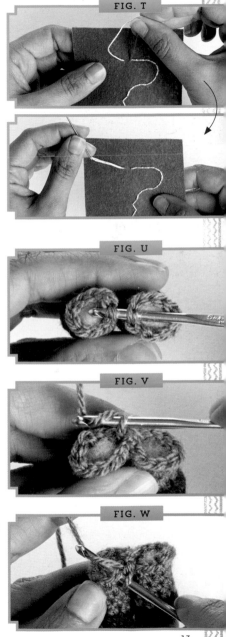

FIG. T

FIG. U

FIG. V

FIG. W

JUDY HOPPS

Determined to prove that she is more than just a cute bunny, Officer Hopps makes up for her lack of physical strength with her quick wits. Though her fellow officers don't take her seriously initially, the first rabbit of the Zootopia Police Department soon earns a place among the finest of the force.

FINISHED SIZE: ABOUT 5.25"

MATERIALS

- Gray DK yarn
- Cream DK yarn
- Pink DK yarn
- Black DK yarn
- Blue DK yarn
- Pair of black plastic safety eyes (6mm)
- Pink embroidery floss
- Black embroidery floss
- Yellow embroidery floss
- Stuffing
- D/3 crochet hook (3.25mm)
- Large needle
- Small sewing needle (optional)

HEAD

- Start with gray yarn.

Rnd 1: make a magic ring and sc 6 (6)

Rnd 2: inc 6 (12)

Rnd 3: [inc, sc] six times (18)

Rnds 4–5: sc in each st (18)

Rnd 6: [inc, sc 8] two times (20)

Rnd 7: sc 6, *change to cream,* sc in the **same** st as the previous sc, work 3 sc in the next st, sc, *change to gray,* sc in the **same** st as the previous sc, sc 12 (24) **(FIG. A)**

FIG. A

Rnd 8: sc 5, *change to cream,* sc, invdec, sc, invdec, sc, *change to gray,* sc 12 (22)

Rnd 9: sc 5, *change to cream,* invdec, sc, invdec, *change to gray,* sc 12 (20)

- Attach the safety eyes between rnds 6 and 7, one stitch from the edge of the cream patch.

Rnd 10: [invdec, sc] six times, invdec (13)

- Stuff the head.

FIG. B

Rnd 11: sc, invdec 6 (7)

- Fasten off and close the remaining hole.
- With gray yarn, embroider 3–4 short horizontal stitches over the top middle of the cream patch to build up the nose bridge. **(FIG. B)** Use 2 strands of pink floss to outline the nose and mouth, then add several more stitches to the nose to make the lines thicker than the mouth. Embroider eyelashes with a single strand of black floss. **(FIG. C)** (For these fine details, a small sewing needle might be more suitable than the large yarn needle.)

FIG. C

INNER EARS (MAKE 2)

- Use pink yarn.

Row 1: ch 8 and, working into the back ridge of chains, sc in the 2nd ch from hook, dc 3, hdc, sc 2, and fasten off (7)

EARS (MAKE 2)

- Use gray yarn.

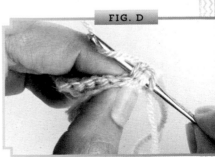
FIG. D

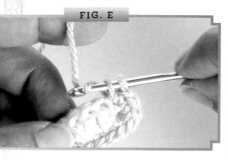
FIG. E

Row 1: ch 8, and working into the back ridge of the chains, sc in the 2nd ch from hook, dc 3, hdc, sc 2. Ch 1 and turn (7)

Row 2: hold a pink inner ear in front of the gray ear (wrong sides together), and work the row through both layers. **(FIG. D—PAGE 15)** Sc 6, work 3 sc in the next st. Skip the turning chains at the ear tip, work 3 sc in the next st, sc 6 (18) **(FIG. E)**

- Fasten off leaving a long end, weave in the other yarn ends. Sew the ears to the head behind rnd 2. **(FIG. F)**

FIG. F

LEGS (MAKE 2)

- Start with gray yarn.

Rnd 1: make a magic ring and sc 5 (5)

Rnd 2: inc 5 (10)

- Change to black yarn.

Rnd 3: sc in each st (10)

Rnd 4: sc 3, invdec 2, sc 3 (8)

Rnd 5: sc 3, invdec, sc 3 (7)

- Change to blue yarn.

Rnds 6–7: sc in each st (7)

Rnd 8: inc, sc 6 (8)

Rnd 9: sc 4, inc, sc 3 (9)

- Sl st in next st and fasten off. Stuff the legs.

FIG. G

BODY

- Start with blue yarn.

Rnd 1: join the legs (see page 13) and sc around (16)

Rnd 2: [inc, sc 7] two times (18)

Rnd 3: sc in each st (18)

Rnd 4: [sc 4, invdec, sc 3] two times (16)

Rnd 5: sc in each st (16)

Rnd 6: [sc 6, invdec] two times (14)

- Change to black yarn.

Rnds 7–9: sc in each st (14)

Rnd 10: [invdec, sc 5] two times (12)

- Change to blue yarn. Stuff the body.

FIG. H

Rnd 11: [sc, invdec] four times (8)

- Sl st in next st and fasten off, leaving a long yarn end.
- For her belt, embroider a chain stitch line between rnds 4 & 5 with black yarn. **(FIG. G)**
- Sew the head to the body.

ARMS (MAKE 2)

- Start with gray yarn.

Rnd 1: make a magic ring and sc 6 (6)

Rnd 2: inc, sc 5 (7)

- Change to black yarn.

Rnds 3-6: sc in each st (7)

- Change to blue yarn.

Rnds 7-11: sc in each st (7)

- Sl st in next st and fasten off, leaving a long yarn end.
- Sew the arms to the body.

- With six strands of yellow floss and chain stitches, embroider a badge to Judy's chest. **(FIG. H)**

KNEE PADS (MAKE 2)

- Use gray yarn.

Row 1: ch 2 and, working in the back ridge of chains, sc in 2nd ch from hook, sl st in the same ch, and fasten off, leaving a long yarn end.

- Sew the knee pads to the legs.

TAIL

- Use gray yarn.

Rnd 1: make a magic ring and sc 6 (6)

Rnds 2-3: sc in each st (6)

- Sl st in next st and fasten off, leaving a long yarn end. Sew the tail to the body, just under the belt.

NICK WILDE

Tired of fighting the shifty fox stereotype, Nick decided to embrace it and became a scam artist, hiding his vulnerability behind wisecracks and nonchalance. Originally reluctant to help Judy, he stands up for her when he realizes they have more in common than he first thought.

FINISHED SIZE: ABOUT 5.5"

MATERIALS

- Orange DK yarn
- Cream DK yarn
- Brown DK yarn
- Beige DK yarn
- Green DK yarn
- Pair of black plastic safety eyes (6mm)
- Purple embroidery floss
- Black embroidery floss
- Indigo embroidery floss
- Stuffing
- D/3 crochet hook (3.25mm)
- Large needle

HEAD

• Start with orange yarn.

Rnd 1: make a magic ring and sc 6 (6)

Rnd 2: inc 6 (12)

Rnd 3: [sc, inc] six times (18)

Rnd 4: [inc, sc 5] three times (21)

Rnds 5–6: sc in each st (21)

Rnd 7: [inc, sc 6] three times (24)

Rnd 8: sc 11, *change to cream, sc 6, change to orange,* sc 7 (24)

Rnd 9: sc 10, *change to cream, sc 8, change to orange,* sc 6 (24)

Rnd 10: sc 11, *change to cream, sc 7, change to orange,* sc 6 (24)

Rnd 11: [invdec, sc] three times, invdec, *change to cream,* [sc, invdec] two times, sc, *change to orange,* [invdec, sc] two times (16)

• Attach safety eyes between rnds 6 and 7, above the corners of the cream patch. Stuff the head.

Rnd 12: invdec 8 (8)

• Fasten off and close the remaining hole.

MUZZLE

• Use cream yarn.

Rnd 1: make a magic ring and sc 6 (6)

Rnd 2: sc in each st (6)

Rnd 3: [inc, sc 2] two times (8)

Rnd 4: sc in each st (8)

• Sl st in next st and fasten off, leaving a long yarn end. Stuff the muzzle and sew it to the head at the top of the cream patch. **(FIG. A)**

MUZZLE STRIPE

• Use orange yarn.

Row 1: ch 4, working in the back ridge of chains sc in 2nd ch from hook, hdc, dc (3)

• Fasten off, leaving a long yarn end, and sew the stripe on the top of the muzzle.

FIG. A

FIG. B

FIG. C

19

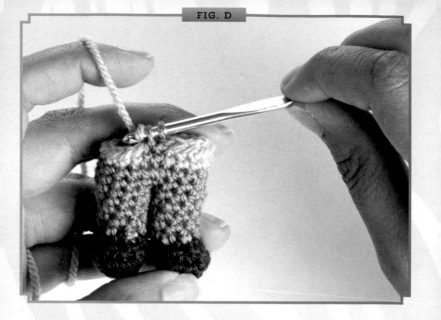

FIG. D

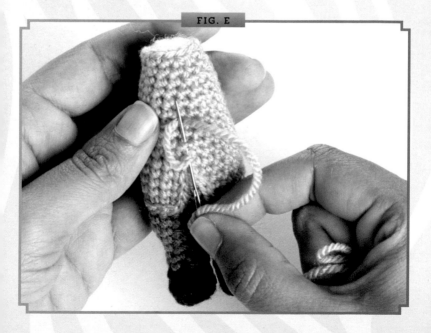

FIG. E

EARS (MAKE 2)

• Start with brown yarn.

Rnd 1: make a magic ring and sc 4 (4)

Rnd 2: [inc, sc] two times (6)

Rnd 3: [inc, sc 2] two times (8)

Rnd 4: [inc, sc 3] two times (10)

Rnd 5: [inc, sc 4] two times (12)

• Change to orange.

Rnd 6: sc in each st (12)

• Sl st in next st and fasten off, leaving a long yarn end. Flatten the ear, then push the corners together so that the base becomes C shaped. Sew the ears to the head—they should be behind the midline when looked at from the top. **(FIG. B—PAGE 19)**

• Embroider the nose with 6 strands of purple floss. Use 2 strands of black floss to embroider the mouth. With orange yarn, embroider 2–3 slanted stitches over the eyes to create the eyelids. **(FIG. C—PAGE 19)**

LEGS (MAKE 2)

• Start with brown yarn.

Rnd 1: make a magic ring and sc 6 (6)

Rnd 2: inc 6 (12)

Rnd 3: sc in each st (12)

Rnd 4: sc 3, invdec 3, sc 3 (9)

• Change to beige.

Rnd 5: sc 4, invdec, sc 3 (8)

Rnds 6–7: sc in each st (8)

Rnd 8: [sc 3, inc] two times (10)

Rnd 9: sc in each st (10)

• Sl st in next st and fasten off. Stuff the legs.

BODY

• Start with beige yarn.

Rnd 1: join the legs (see page 13) and sc around (18)

Rnd 2: [inc, sc 8] two times (20)

• Change to green.

Rnds 3–4: sc 10, *change to beige*, sc 2, *change to green*, sc 8 (20) **(FIG. D)**

Rnd 5: sc 11, *change to beige*, sc 1, *change to green*, sc 8 (20)

Rnds 6–8: sc in each st (20)

Rnd 9: [invdec, sc 8] two times (18)

Rnds 10–12: sc in each st (18)

Rnd 13: [invdec, sc 4] three times (15)

Rnds 14–15: sc in each st (15)

Rnd 16: [invdec, sc 3] three times (12)

• Stuff the body.

Rnd 17: [invdec, sc] four times (8)

• Sl st in next st and fasten off, leaving a long yarn end.

• With green yarn, embroider a chain stitch line around the edges of the shirt, then continue the line up to the neck. **(FIG. E)**

• Sew the head to the body.

ARMS (MAKE 2)

• Start with brown yarn.

Rnd 1: make a magic ring and sc 6 (6)

Rnd 2: [inc, sc 2] two times (8)

Rnd 3: sc in each st (8)

Rnd 4: sc 6, invdec (7)

Rnds 5–6: sc in each st (7)

• Change to orange.

Rnds 7–8: sc in each st (7)

• Change to green.

Rnd 9: sc 3, inc, sc 3 (8)

Rnds 10–14: sc in each st (8)

• Sl st in next st and fasten off, leaving a long yarn end.

• To make the transition between brown and orange smoother, unravel a length of orange yarn and use the separated strands to embroider short straight stitches near the edge of the brown area. **(FIG. F—PAGE 22)**

• Sew the arms to the body.

FIG. F

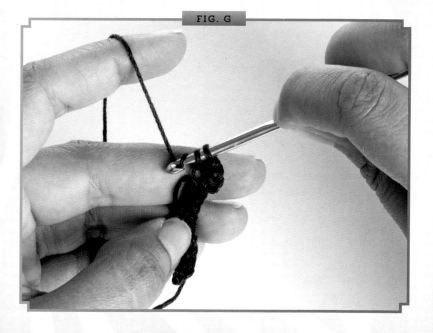

FIG. G

TAIL

- Start with brown yarn.

Rnd 1: make a magic ring and sc 6 (6)

Rnd 2: sc in each st (6)

Rnd 3: sc 2, inc 2, sc 2 (8)

Rnd 4: sc 3, inc 2, sc 3 (10)

Rnd 5: sc in each st (10)

Rnd 6: sc 4, inc 2, sc 4 (12)

Rnd 7: sc in each st (12)

- Change to orange.

Rnds 8–11: sc in each st (12)

Rnd 12: sc 5, invdec, sc 5 (11)

Rnds 13–14: sc in each st (11)

Rnd 15: sc 5, invdec, sc 4 (10)

- Stuff the tail lightly.

Rnd 16: invdec 5 (5)

- Fasten off, leaving a long yarn end. To make the color transition smoother, embroider short stitches with a separated ply of orange yarn near the edge of the brown area.

- Sew the tail to the body.

TIE

- Use indigo embroidery floss.

Row 1: using six strands of embroidery floss, ch 11 and working in the back ridge of chains, sc in 2nd ch from hook, hdc 5, sc 3, sl st. Ch 1, hdc 2 in the same ch as the sl st, ch 1 and sl st again in the same ch as the hdc stitches. **(FIG. G)**

- Fasten off, leaving a long yarn end, and sew the tie to the neck of the doll.

3

CHIEF BOGO

A seasoned ZPD officer, Chief Bogo is cynical and gruff but still passionate for justice, and he cares deeply for his officers. He has a secret he'd rather hide from his subordinates though: he's Gazelle's biggest fan!

FINISHED SIZE: ABOUT 8"

MATERIALS

- Medium gray DK yarn
- Dark gray DK yarn
- Brown DK yarn
- Beige DK yarn
- Black DK yarn
- Blue DK yarn
- Pair of black plastic safety eyes (6mm)

- White felt
- Yellow embroidery floss
- 12" pipe cleaner and a wire cutter
- Stuffing
- D/3 crochet hook (3.25mm)
- B/1 crochet hook (2.25mm)
- Large needle

EYE PREPARATION

Cut a ½" square of white felt and make a hole in the middle. Push the eye stem through and cut the felt off right around the eye. **(FIG. A)** Repeat for the second eye.

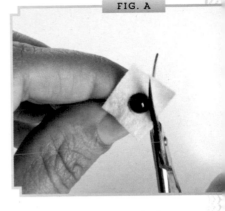

FIG. A

HEAD

- Start with medium gray yarn and a D/3 hook.

Rnd 1: make a magic ring and sc 8 (8)

Rnd 2: inc 8 (16)

Rnd 3: [inc, sc] eight times (24)

Rnd 4: [sc 2, invdec, sc 2] four times (20)

- Change to dark gray.

Rnds 5-7: sc in each st (20)

Rnd 8: sc 8, inc 4, sc 8 (24)

Rnd 9: sc 8, [inc, sc] four times, sc 8 (28)

Rnd 10: [sc 3, inc, sc 3] four times (32)

Rnds 11-16: sc in each st (32)

Rnd 17: [sc 14, invdec] two times (30)

Rnd 18: [invdec, sc 3] six times (24)

Rnd 19: [invdec, sc] eight times (16)

- Attach safety eyes between rnds 8 and 9, about 4 st apart (the increases are on the top side of the head). **(FIG. B)** Stuff the head.

Rnd 20: invdec 8 (8)

- Fasten off and close the remaining hole.

FIG. B

NOSE

- Use brown yarn and a D/3 hook.

Row 1: ch 4. Working in the back ridge of chains, sc in 2nd ch from loop, sc 2. Ch 2, turn (3)

Row 2: hdc, sc, hdc, ch 2 and sl st in the same st as the last hdc

- Fasten off, leaving a long yarn end. Sew the nose to the head so that the bottom (the foundation chain) is level with the center of the magic ring.

- Embroider a mouth and eyebrows with black yarn. **(FIG. C)**

FIG. C

FIG. D

EARS (MAKE 2)

• Use dark gray yarn and a D/3 hook.

Row 1: ch 7. Working in the back ridge of chains, sc in 2nd ch from hook, hdc, dc 3, (hdc, sc) in the last ch. Ch 1 and turn (7)

Row 2: sl st 7, ch 2 and skip the chain at the tip of the ear, then crocheting into the unworked loops of the foundation chain, sl st 6

• Fasten off, leaving a long yarn end, and sew the ears to the head between rnds 14 and 15; the upper corner should be level with the bottom of the eyes. **(FIG. D)**

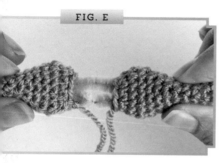

FIG. E

HORNS (MAKE 2)

• Use beige yarn and a D/3 hook.

Rnd 1: make a magic ring and sc 4 (4)

Rnd 2: inc, sc 3 (5)

Rnd 3: inc, sc 4 (6)

Rnds 4-7: sc in each st (6)

Rnd 8: inc, sc 5 (7)

Rnds 9-10: sc in each st (7)

Rnd 11: inc, sc 6 (8)

Rnd 12: sc in each st (8)

Rnd 13: [inc, sc 3] two times (10)

Rnd 14: sc in each st (10)

Rnd 15: [inc, sc 4] two times (12)

Rnd 16: [inc, sc 5] two times (14)

Rnd 17: sc in each st (14)

Rnd 18: invdec 7 (7)

FIG. F

• Sl st in next st and fasten off, leaving a long yarn end. Flatten the horn.

• Use the shaft of your hook to measure the length of the hole inside the horn, and cut a piece of pipe cleaner four times as long. Fold both ends to the middle (so the sharp ends won't poke out at the tips), then pull the horns over this pipe cleaner frame. **(FIG. E)** Insert a small bit of stuffing into the wide area on each

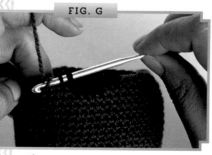

FIG. G

side, then sew together the two sides. Stitching through the seam at the middle, sew the horns to the top of the head, then bend them into the right shape. **(FIG. F)**

LEGS (MAKE 2)

• Start with black yarn and a D/3 hook.

Rnd 1: make a magic ring and sc 6 (6)

Rnd 2: inc 6 (12)

Rnd 3: working in BLO this round, sc in each st (12)

Rnd 4: sc 4, invdec 2, sc 4 (10)

• Change to dark gray.

Rnd 5: sc in each st (10)

• Change to blue.

Rnds 6-8: sc in each st (10)

Rnd 9: [sc 2, inc, sc 2] two times (12)

Rnd 10: [inc, sc 5] two times (14)

Rnd 11: [sc 3, inc, sc 3] two times (16)

• Sl st in next st and fasten off. Stuff the legs.

BODY

• Use blue yarn and a D/3 hook.

Rnd 1: join the legs (see page 13) and sc around (30)

Rnd 2: [inc, sc 14] two times (32)

Rnds 3-5: sc in each st (32)

Rnd 6: [inc, sc 15] two times (34)

Rnds 7-11: sc in each st (34)

Rnd 12: sc 3, inc, [sc 5, inc] five times (40)

Rnd 13: [sc 9, inc] four times (44)

Rnd 14: sc in each st (44)

Rnd 15: [inc, sc 21] two times (46)

Rnds 16-26: sc in each st (46)

Extra stitches: sc as many as necessary so you can start the next rnd at the middle of the back (see Fig. A, page 38)

Rnd 27: sc 10, invdec, sc 9, change

to black, sc 4, change to blue, sc 9, invdec, sc 10 (44)

Rnd 28: sc 6, invdec 5, sc 2, change to black, sc 8, change to blue, sc 2, invdec 5, sc 6 (34) **(FIG. G)**

• Change to dark gray.

Rnd 29: sc 6, invdec, sc, invdec, sc 12, invdec, sc, invdec, sc 6 (30)

Rnd 30: [invdec, sc 3] six times (24)

Rnd 31: sc in each st (24)

• Sl st in next st and fasten off, leaving a long yarn end.

• Stuff the body (make sure to emphasize the wide shoulders), but leave the neck unstuffed.

• Sew the head to the body. When you are about three quarters done, pause to stuff the neck, then close the remaining gap.

BELT

• Use black yarn and a D/3 hook.

Row 1: ch 35 (or as many as necessary to reach around the body, plus 1). Working in the back ridge of chains, sc in the 2nd ch from hook and in each subsequent ch, fasten off, leaving a long yarn end

• Wrap the piece around the waist over rnd 7, sew the ends together at the back, then stitch the belt to the body at several places.

COLLAR (MAKE 2)

• Use blue yarn and a D/3 hook.

Row 1: ch 8, sl st in the 2nd ch from hook, skip 2 ch, dc, hdc, sc, sl st (5) **(FIG. H—PAGE 28)**

• Fasten off, leaving a long yarn end.

• Sew the collar pieces to the body, leaving the 4 black st from rnd 27 free between them.

• With blue yarn and chain stitches, embroider a wide V shape to frame

FIG. H

the black undershirt, then a vertical line connecting the bottom of the V to the belt. **(FIG. I)**

ARMS (MAKE 2)

· Start with black yarn and a D/3 hook.

Rnd 1: make a magic ring and sc 5 (5)

Rnd 2: inc 5 (10)

Rnd 3: working in BLO this rnd, sc in each st (10)

· Change to dark gray.

Rnd 4: sc 4, invdec, sc 4 (9)

Rnds 5-6: sc in each st (9)

Rnd 7: [inc, sc 2] three times (12)

Rnds 8-9: sc in each st (12)

Rnd 10: [inc, sc 5] two times (14)

Rnds 11-13: sc in each st (14)

Rnd 14: [invdec, sc 5] two times (12)

Rnd 15: [inc, sc 3] three times (15)

Rnd 16: sc in each st (15)

· Change to blue.

Rnd 17: [sc 4, inc] three times (18)

Rnds 18-23: sc in each st (18)

Rnd 24: [invdec, sc] six times (12)

· Stuff the forearm tightly but leave the upper arm loosely stuffed.

Rnd 25: invdec 6 (6)

· Fasten off and close the remaining hole.

· Pin the arms to the body. Flatten the shoulder area towards the chest and sew the arm to the body. **(FIG. J)**

TAIL

· Use dark gray yarn and a D/3 hook.

Row 1: ch 7. Working in the back ridge of chains, sc in the 2nd ch from hook, sc 5 (6)

· Fasten off, leaving a long yarn end.

· To add a tuft, cut a 2" piece of black yarn. Insert your hook through the tip of the tail, grab the middle of the

FIG. I

FIG. J

SEWING LINE

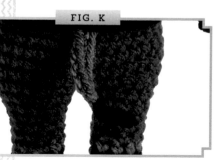

FIG. K

yarn piece and pull through to make a loop, then pull the yarn ends through this loop. Repeat with a second piece of yarn, then cut the tuft to ½" in length.

- Sew the tail to the body just under the belt. **(FIG. K)**

BADGE

- Use yellow embroidery floss and B/1 hook.

Rnd 1: make a magic ring and sc 2, ch 1, hdc 3, ch 1, hdc 3, ch 1, sc 1 (12 st including chains)

- Sl st in the top of the next st and fasten off, leaving a long end.
- Sew the badge to the doll's chest. (The chain between the hdc stitches is the bottom point of the badge.)

4

OFFICER CLAWHAUSER

Officer Clawhauser's friendly smile and helpful disposition immediately puts ZPD's visitors at ease. Enthusiastic and cheery overall, his two greatest passions in life are pop star Gazelle and doughnuts covered in sprinkles.

FINISHED SIZE: ABOUT 6.5"

MATERIALS

- Camel DK yarn
- Cream DK yarn
- Black DK yarn
- Blue DK yarn
- Pink DK yarn
- Brown DK yarn
- Pair of black plastic safety eyes (6mm)
- Purple embroidery floss
- Black embroidery floss
- Yellow embroidery floss
- Black fabric marker
- Stuffing
- D/3 crochet hook (3.25mm)
- B/1 crochet hook (2.25mm)
- Large needle

HEAD

· Use camel yarn and a D/3 hook.

Rnd 1: make a magic ring and sc 6 (6)

Rnd 2: inc 6 (12)

Rnd 3: [sc, inc] six times (18)

Rnd 4: [inc, sc 5] three times (21)

Rnds 5-7: sc in each st (21)

Rnd 8: [inc 2, sc] seven times (35)

Rnd 9: [sc 4, inc] seven times (42)

Rnds 10-14: sc in each st (42)

Rnd 15: [invdec, sc 5] six times (36)

Rnd 16: [invdec, sc 2] nine times (27)

Rnd 17: [sc, invdec] nine times (18)

· Attach safety eyes between rnds 6 and 7, about 3 st apart. Stuff the head.

Rnd 18: invdec 9 (9)

· Fasten off and close the remaining hole.

MUZZLE PATCH

· Start with cream yarn and a D/3 hook.

Rnd 1: make a magic ring and sc 6 (6)

Rnd 2: inc 6 (12)

Rnd 3: [sc 3, inc 3] two times (18)

Rnd 4: sc 3, [sc, inc] three times, *change to camel*, sc 3, *change to cream*, [inc, sc] three times (24)

· Sl st in next st and fasten off, leaving a long yarn end. Pin the piece to the head—the camel stitches should be under the eyes. Sew this part on with a length of camel yarn, then sew the rest of the patch using the cream yarn end. **(FIG. A)**

· With 6 strands of purple floss, embroider the nose, then use 2 strands of black floss to create the mouth. With black yarn, embroider "tear marks" from the bottom of the eyes to the sides of the muzzle. **(FIG. B)**

EARS (MAKE 2)

· Start with black yarn and a D/3 hook.

Rnd 1: make a magic ring and sc 6 (6)

FIG. A

FIG. B

FIG. C

Rnd 2: inc, sc 3, *change to camel*, sc in the **same** st as the previous sc, sc 1, *change to black*, sc 1 (8)

Rnd 3: sc 5, *change to camel*, sc 3 (8)

• Change to black.

Rnd 4: sc 4, sl st (5 st plus 3 unworked)

• Fasten off, leaving long ends of both camel and black yarn. Flatten the ears and sew them to the sides of the head using the matching tail. **(FIG. C—PAGE 31)**

LEGS (MAKE 2)

• Start with camel yarn and a D/3 hook.

Rnd 1: make a magic ring and sc 6 (6)

Rnd 2: inc 6 (12)

Rnd 3: [inc, sc 2] four times (16)

Rnd 4: sc in each st (16)

Rnd 5: sc 4, invdec 4, sc 4 (12)

• Change to blue.

Rnd 6: sc in each st (12)

Rnd 7: [inc, sc 3] three times (15)

Rnd 8: sc in each st (15)

Rnd 9: [sc 2, inc, sc 2] three times (18)

Rnd 10: sc in each st (18)

Rnd 11: [inc, sc 5] three times (21)

• Sl st in next st and fasten off. Stuff the legs.

BODY

• Start with blue yarn and a D/3 hook.

Rnd 1: join the legs (see page 13) and sc around (40)

Rnd 2: [inc, sc 9] four times (44)

Rnd 3: [sc 5, inc, sc 5] four times (48)

Rnds 4–6: sc in each st (48)

Rnd 7: sc 19, [inc, sc 4] three times, sc 14 (51)

Rnds 8–13: sc in each st (51)

Extra stitches: sc as many as necessary to start the next rnd at the middle of the back (see page 38—Fig. A)

Rnd 14: sc 20, [invdec, sc 3] three times, sc 16 (48)

Rnd 15: [invdec, sc 10] four times (44)

Rnds 16–18: sc in each st (44)

Rnd 19: [invdec, sc 9] four times (40)

Rnd 20: [sc 4, invdec, sc 4] four times (36)

Rnd 21: [sc 5, invdec, sc 5] three times (33)

Rnd 22: [invdec, sc 9] three times (30)

Rnd 23: [sc 4, invdec, sc 4] three times (27)

Rnd 24: [invdec, sc 7] three times (24)

• Sl st in next st and fasten off, leaving a long yarn end. Stuff the body and flatten it slightly, so that it is oval rather than round in cross-section.

• Sew the head to the body. (Pause when there is only a small gap left and check if you need to add more stuffing to the neck.)

BELT

• Use black yarn and a D/3 hook.

Row 1: ch 49 (or as many as necessary to reach around the body at rnd 7, plus 1). Working in the back ridge of chains, sc in the 2nd ch from hook and in each subsequent ch, fasten off, leaving a long yarn end

• Wrap the piece around the body over rnd 7, sew the ends together at the back, then stitch the belt to the body at several places.

ARMS (MAKE 2)

• Start with camel yarn and a D/3 hook.

Rnd 1: make a magic ring and sc 6 (6)

Rnd 2: inc 6 (12)

Rnds 3–5: sc in each st (12)

• Change to blue.

Rnds 6–20: sc in each st (12)

Rnd 21: [invdec, sc 4] two times (10)

• Sl st in next st and fasten off, leaving a long yarn end. Stuff the arms lightly, then sew them to the body.

TIE

· Use black yarn and a D/3 hook.

Row 1: ch 11 and working in the back ridge of chains, sc in 2nd ch from hook, hdc 5, sc 3, sl st. Ch 1, hdc 2 in the same ch as the sl st, ch 1 and sl st again in the same ch as the hdc stitches

· Sew the "tie knot" to the neck, then stitch the tip down to the belly. With blue yarn and chain stitches, embroider a line between the belt and the tie. Fasten off, leaving a long yarn end. **(FIG. D)**

FIG. D

COLLAR (MAKE 2)

· Use blue yarn and a D/3 hook.

Row 1: ch 8, sl st in the 2nd ch from hook, skip 2 ch, dc, hdc, sc, sl st (5)

· Fasten off, leaving a long yarn end. Sew the collar pieces to the neck beside the tie knot. **(FIG. E)**

FIG. E

TAIL

· Start with black yarn and a D/3 hook.

Rnd 1: make a magic ring and sc 7 (7)

Rnds 2-4: sc in each st (7)

· Change to camel.

Rnd 5: sc in each st (7)

· Change to black.

Rnd 6: sc in each st (7)

· Change to camel.

Rnd 7: sc in each st (7)

· Change to black.

Rnd 8: sc in each st (7) **(FIG. F)**

· Change to camel.

Rnds 9-25: sc in each st (7)

· Sl st in next st and fasten off, leaving a long yarn end. Sew the tail to the bottom just under the belt.

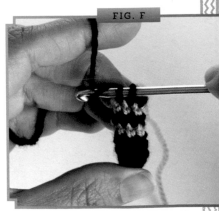

FIG. F

BADGE

· Use yellow embroidery floss and B/1 hook.

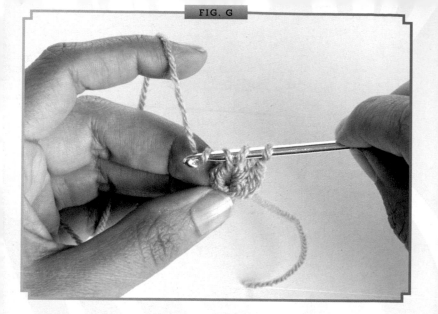

FIG. G

FIG. H

Rnd 1: make a magic ring and sc 2, ch 1, hdc 3, ch 1, hdc 3, ch 1, sc 1 (12 st including chains)

- Sl st in the top of the next st and fasten off, leaving a long end.
- Sew the badge to the doll's chest. (The chain between the hdc stitches is the bottom point of the badge.)

SPOTS

- Use a fabric marker to paint black spots on the head, paws, and tail. You won't be able to heat fix the paint, but amigurumi figures don't need regular washing, so it shouldn't be a problem. If you are worried about the color running should it ever get wet, try it first on a separate test piece (most fabric markers won't run).

DOUGHNUT

- Make 1 with brown yarn and 1 with pink yarn.

Rnd 1: using a D/3 hook, ch 5, and sl st in the first ch to create a ring. Ch 2, and inserting your hook through the central hole rather than individual chains, hdc 9 into the ring (9 st not including chains) **(FIG. G)**

- Sl st in the top of the first hdc and fasten off, leaving a long yarn end on the pink piece. Weave in the other ends. Hold the two pieces with wrong sides together, and sew the outer edges together with the pink yarn end.
- Sew the finished doughnut to the hand.

SNEAKY DOUGHNUT

- Start with brown yarn and a D/3 hook.

Row 1: ch 5, sc in 2nd ch from hook, sc 3. *Change to pink*, ch 2 and turn (4)

Row 2: hdc 4 (4)

- Fasten off, leaving a long yarn end. Weave in the other ends. Fold the piece in half and tuck it between the head and the collar to make the impression of a half-hidden doughnut. Sew the doughnut to the neck. **(FIG. H)**

MAYOR LIONHEART

Mayor Lionheart coined the slogan that has been Judy's lifelong inspiration: "*In Zootopia, anyone can be anything.*" While his actions might not have been entirely selfless, the mayor's Mammal Inclusion Initiative helped many young animals to pursue their dream careers rather than stick to conventions.

FINISHED SIZE: ABOUT 6.5"

MATERIALS

- Camel DK yarn
- Blue DK yarn
- Cream DK yarn
- Red DK yarn
- Beige DK yarn
- Pair of black plastic safety eyes (6mm)
- Purple embroidery floss

- Black embroidery floss
- White felt
- Stuffing
- D/3 crochet hook (3.25mm)
- Large needle
- Piece of cardboard

LEGS (MAKE 2)

• Start with camel yarn.

Rnd 1: make a magic ring and sc 6 (6)

Rnd 2: inc 6 (12)

Rnd 3: [inc, sc 2] four times (16)

Rnd 4: sc in each st (16)

Rnd 5: sc 6, invdec 2, sc 6 (14)

• Change to blue.

Rnd 6: sc 5, invdec 2, sc 5 (12)

Rnds 7-8: sc in each st (12)

Rnd 9: [inc, sc 5] two times (14)

Rnds 10-12: sc in each st (14)

Rnd 13: [inc, sc 6] two times (16)

• Sl st in next st and fasten off. Stuff the legs.

BODY AND HEAD

• Start with blue yarn.

Rnd 1: join the legs (see page 13) and sc around (30)

Rnd 2: [inc, sc 9] three times (33)

Rnds 3-5: sc in each st (33)

Rnd 6: [inc, sc 10] three times (36)

Rnds 7-11: sc in each st (36)

Rnd 12: [inc, sc 8] four times (40)

Rnd 13: sc in each st (40)

Rnd 14: [inc, sc 19] two times (42)

Rnds 15-24: sc in each st (42)

Extra stitches: sc as many as necessary to start the next rnd at the middle of the back **(FIG. A—PAGE 38)**

Rnd 25: sc 5, invdec 6, sc 9, invdec 6, sc 4 (30)

• Change to camel.

Rnd 26: sc 5, invdec 3, sc 9, invdec 3, sc 4 (24)

Rnds 27-28: sc in each st (24)

• Stuff the body.

Rnd 29: [inc, sc 3] six times (30)

Rnd 30: [sc 9, inc] three times (33)

Rnds 31-35: sc in each st (33)

Rnd 36: [invdec, sc 9] three times (30)

Rnds 37-39: sc in each st (30)

Rnd 40: [invdec, sc 3] six times (24)

Rnd 41: [sc 2, invdec] six times (18)

• Attach safety eyes between rnds 35 and 36, about 6 st apart.

Rnd 42: [invdec, sc] six times (12)

• Stuff the head.

Rnd 43: invdec 6 (6)

• Fasten off and close the remaining hole.

MUZZLE

• Start with cream yarn.

Rnd 1: make a magic ring and sc 6 (6)

Rnd 2: inc 6 (12)

Rnd 3: [inc, sc] six times (18)

Rnd 4: sc 8, invdec, sc 8 (17)

Rnd 5: sc 8, invdec, sc 7 (16)

• Change to camel.

Rnds 6-7: sc in each st (16)

• Sl st in next st and fasten off, leaving a long yarn end.

• The decreases should be at the bottom, forming a small chin. Stuff the muzzle and sew it to the head so that the top is at rnd 34. **(FIG. B—PAGE 38)**

MUZZLE STRIPE

• Use camel yarn.

Row 1: ch 5. Working in the back ridge of the chain, hdc in the 3rd ch from hook, hdc, (hdc, sc) in the last ch, then continue working on the other side of the foundation chain: (sc, hdc) in the same ch, hdc 2 (8) **(FIG. C—PAGE 38)**

• Ch 2, sl st in the same ch as the last hdc, then fasten off, leaving a long yarn end.

• Sew the stripe to the top of the muzzle.

• Embroider the nose with 6 strands of purple floss, then create the mouth

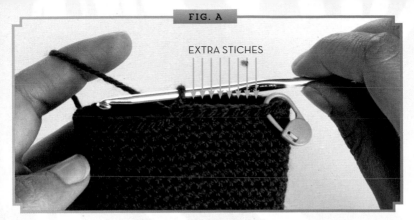

FIG. A

EXTRA STICHES

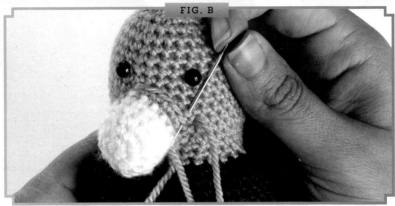

FIG. B

FIG. C

with 2 strands of black floss. Use 6 strands of black floss to embroider eyebrows. **(FIG. D)**

EARS (MAKE 2)
• Use camel yarn.

Rnd 1: make a magic ring and sc 6 (6)

Rnd 2: [inc, sc] three times (9)

Rnds 3-4: sc in each st (9)

• Sl st in next st and fasten off, leaving a long yarn end. Flatten the ears and sew them to the sides of the head, the lower corner should be level with the eyes. **(FIG. E)**

SHIRT AND TIE
• Cut out the shirt triangle from felt using the template on page 75. Pin it to the doll (the top should be at the border between blue and camel). With red yarn, embroider the tie over the felt, stitching through the crochet fabric too—this will also attach the shirt to the chest. **(FIG. F)**

ARMS (MAKE 2)
• Start with camel yarn.

Rnd 1: make a magic ring and sc 6 (6)

Rnd 2: inc 6 (12)

Rnds 3-5: sc in each st (12)

• Change to blue.

Rnds 6-22: sc in each st (12)

Rnd 23: [invdec, sc 4] two times (10)

• Sl st in next st and fasten off, leaving a long yarn end. Stuff the arms lightly, then sew them to the body 2 rnds below the color change. **(FIG. G)**

LAPELS (MAKE ONE A AND ONE B)
• Use blue yarn.

A: Ch 14, sl st in 2nd ch from hook, sl st, sc 2, hdc 2, dc 2, ch 3, sl st, ch 3, dc 3, sc, fasten off, leaving a long yarn end. **(FIG. H—PAGE 40)**

FIG. D

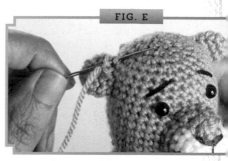
FIG. E

FIG. F

FIG. G

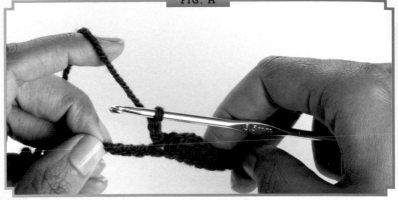

FIG. H

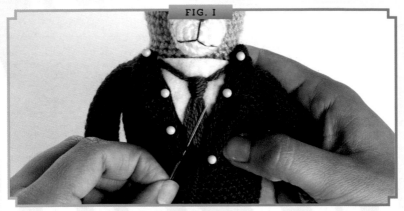

FIG. I

FIG. J

B: Ch 14, sc in 2nd ch from hook, dc 3, ch 3, sl st, ch 3, dc 2, hdc 2, sc 2, sl st 2, fasten off, leaving a long yarn end.

- Sew the lapels to the sides of the shirt triangle. **(FIG. I)** To add further details to the suit, embroider a chain stitch line with blue yarn above rnd 7 of the body, then a vertical line connecting it to the lapels.

TAIL

- Use camel yarn.

Rnd 1: make a magic ring and sc 6 (6)

Rnds 2-26: sc in each st (6)

- Sl st in next st and fasten off, leaving a long yarn end.
- Sew the tail to the body at rnd 8.

TAIL TUFT AND MANE

- Cut a piece of cardboard, 1.5" wide. Wrap beige yarn around the

cardboard and cut the wraps open on one side to get a batch of 3" pieces. Insert your hook through the tip of the tail, grab the middle of the yarn piece and pull through to make a loop, then pull the yarn ends through this loop. Attach more pieces around the tail tip for a full tuft, then cut the strands to an even length.

- For the mane, start attaching the yarn pieces at the neck and work your way up to the crown and then towards the forehead. Attach a strand about every 2nd st, then you can add more if some areas are not sufficiently covered. **(FIG. J)** For a neat finish, trim the bottom of the mane to an even length. If the strands stick up too wildly, you can tame them with hair mousse.

6

ASSISTANT MAYOR BELLWETHER

A tiny, fluffy sheep, Assistant Mayor Bellwether appears sweet and meek, but she holds a bitter grudge against predators. She manipulates the fear of others to reach her ultimate goal.

FINISHED SIZE: ABOUT 5"

MATERIALS

- Cream DK yarn
- Beige DK yarn
- White DK yarn
- Red DK yarn
- Navy blue DK yarn
- Fleecy novelty yarn (or a loopy boucle yarn) in cream
- Pair of black plastic safety eyes (6mm)

- Pink embroidery floss
- Brown embroidery floss
- Black embroidery floss
- Stuffing
- D/3 crochet hook (3.25mm)
- Large needle
- Air erasable fabric marker

HEAD

- Use cream yarn.

Rnd 1: make a magic ring and sc 6 (6)

Rnd 2: inc 6 (12)

Rnd 3: [inc, sc 2] four times (16)

Rnds 4-6: sc in each st (16)

Rnd 7: [invdec, sc 2] four times (12)

Rnd 8: inc 3, sc 6, inc 3 (18)

Rnd 9: sc in each st (18)

- Stuff the bun.

Rnd 10: [inc, sc] three times, sc 6, [sc, inc] three times (24)

Rnd 11: sc in each st (24)

Rnd 12: inc, sc 5, inc, sc 10, inc, sc 6 (27)

Rnds 13-17: sc in each st (27)

Rnd 18: [invdec, sc] nine times (18)

- Attach safety eyes between rnds 11 and 12, 4 st apart (the increases are at the back of the head). Stuff the head.

Rnd 19: invdec 9 (9)

- Fasten off and close the remaining hole.

MUZZLE

- Use cream yarn.

Rnd 1: make a magic ring and sc 6 (6)

Rnd 2: [inc, sc] three times (9)

Rnd 3: sc 5, sl st (6 st, plus 3 unworked)

- Fasten off, leaving a long yarn end.
- Sew the muzzle to the head with the unworked stitches at the top, 1 rnd below the eyes.
- Embroider the mouth and the nose with 2 strands of pink floss.
- Copy the eyeglass template on page 75 to paper and cut it out. Place the template to the face (fitting the hole over the safety eye) and trace it to the head with erasable marker. **(FIG. A)** Use 6 strands of brown floss and chain stitches to embroider the glasses. **(FIG. B)** Work the two sides with

FIG. A

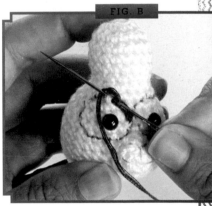

FIG. B

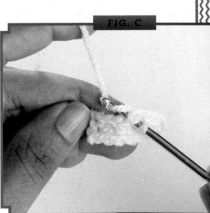

FIG. C

43

FIG. D

FIG. E

FIG. F

separate floss, so if the end result is not symmetrical enough, it is easier to undo one side and start again. Finally, connect the sides with two horizontal stitches.

EARS (MAKE 2)

• Use cream yarn.

Row 1: ch 7. Working in the back ridge of chains, sc in 2nd ch from hook, hdc 4, sc. Ch 1 and turn (6)

Row 2: sl st 6, ch 2 and skip the chain at the tip of the ear, then crocheting into the unworked loops of the foundation chain, sl st 6. **(FIG. C—PAGE 43)**

• Fasten off, leaving a long yarn end, and sew the ears to sides of the head, level with the eyes. **(FIG. D)**

• For a fluffy look, embroider long vertical stitches with the fuzzy novelty yarn, all over the head except the muzzle and around the eyes. **(FIG. E)** Dragging the yarn through the crochet fabric damages the fuzz, so use pieces no longer than about 12".

LEGS (MAKE 2)

• Start with beige yarn.

Rnd 1: make a magic ring and sc 3, hdc 2, sc 3 (8)

Rnd 2: working in BLO this rnd, sc in each st (8)

• Change to cream.

Rnd 3: sc 2, invdec 2, sc 2 (6)

Rnds 4-6: sc in each st (6)

Rnd 7: [inc, sc] three times (9)

Rnds 8-9: sc in each st (9)

• Sl st in next st and fasten off. Stuff the legs.

BODY

• Start with cream yarn.

Rnd 1: join the legs (see page 13, but turn the hooves inwards rather than

outwards) and sc around (16) **(FIG. F)**

Rnd 2: [inc, sc 3] four times (20)

Rnds 3-4: sc in each st (20)

Rnd 5: sc, invdec, sc 14, invdec, sc (18)

• Change to white.

Rnd 6: working in BLO this rnd, sc in each st (18)

Rnd 7: [invdec, sc 7] two times (16)

Rnds 8-9: sc in each st (16)

Rnd 10: [invdec, sc 2] four times (12)

• Sl st in next st and fasten off, leaving a long yarn end. Stuff the body.

SKIRT

• Use red yarn.

• Turn the body upside down so you can work into the free loops from rnd 6. Insert your hook through the first loop, YO and pull up a loop, then ch 1. **(FIG. G—PAGE 46)** This does not count as a stitch; work the first sc in the same loop.

Rnd 1: [sc, inc, sc] 6 times (24)

Rnd 2: sc in each st (24)

Rnd 3: [inc, sc 7] three times (27)

Rnd 4: [sc 4, inc, sc 4] three times (30)

Rnds 5-6: sc in each st (30)

Rnd 7: [inc, sc 9] three times (33)

Rnd 8: sc in each st (33)

• Sl st in next st, fasten off, and weave in yarn ends.

• With 3 strands of black floss, stitch through the body from back to front, then back again leaving a very short, dot-like stitch on the front. **(FIG. H—PAGE 46)** Repeat to cover the visible front of the "shirt" with dots (no problem if you leave messy stitches on the back; the jacket will hide that).

• Sew the head to the body.

JACKET

• Use navy yarn.

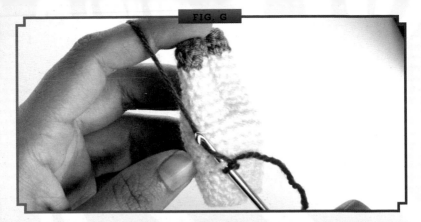

FIG. G

FIG. H

FIG. I

Row 1: ch 13, sc in the 2nd ch from hook, sc 11. Ch 1 and turn (12)

Row 2: [sc, inc, sc] four times. Ch 1 and turn (16)

Row 3: sc in each st. Ch 1 and turn (16)

Row 4: sc 2, inc, sc 10, inc, sc 2. Ch 1 and turn (18)

Row 5: sc in each st. Ch 1 and turn (18)

Row 6: working in BLO this row [sc, inc, sc] six times. Ch 1 and turn (24)

Row 7: sc in each st (24)

· Fasten off and weave in yarn ends.

ARMS (MAKE 2)

· Start with beige yarn.

Rnd 1: make a magic ring and sc 7 (7)

Rnd 2: working in BLO this rnd, sc in each st (7)

· Change to cream.

Rnds 3-5: sc in each st (7)

· Change to navy blue.

Rnds 6-11: sc in each st (7)

· Sl st in next st and fasten off, leaving a long yarn end.

· Wrap the jacket around the torso, then pin and sew the arms in place. Make sure some of your stitches reach down to the body, attaching the arms and the jacket at the same time. **(FIG. I)**

TAIL

· Use cream yarn.

Rnd 1: make a magic ring and sc 5 (5)

Rnds 2-3: sc in each st (5)

· Sl st in next st and fasten off, leaving a long yarn end. Sew the tail to the top of the skirt.

· Optionally, you may also cover the thighs and the tail with fuzzy yarn.

7

FLASH

One of the many sloths working at the DMV (Department of Mammal Vehicles), Flash is unfazed by the tempo of the world around him or the impatience of his clients. Seemingly happy to live his life in slow motion, he has a secret passion for fast cars and street racing.

FINISHED SIZE: ABOUT 5.5"

MATERIALS

- Medium gray DK yarn
- Beige DK yarn
- Green DK yarn
- Ecru DK yarn
- Dark gray DK yarn
- Medium blue DK yarn
- Dark blue DK yarn
- Orange DK yarn

- Pair of flat backed black plastic eyes (6mm), or safety eyes and wire cutter
- Black embroidery floss
- Stuffing
- D/3 crochet hook (3.25mm)
- Large needle
- Fabric or craft glue

LEGS (MAKE 2)

- Start with medium gray yarn.

Rnd 1: make a magic ring and sc 6 (6)

Rnd 2: inc 6 (12)

Rnd 3: sc in each st (12)

- Change to beige.

Rnds 4-5: sc in each st (12)

Rnd 6: [inc, sc 5] two times (14)

Rnds 7-8: sc in each st (14)

Rnd 9: [inc, sc 6] two times (16)

- Sl st in next st and fasten off. Stuff the legs.

BODY AND HEAD

- Start with beige yarn.

Rnd 1: join the legs (see page 13—there is no foot shaping here, so you can join through any two stitches) and sc around (30)

Rnd 2: [inc, sc 14] two times (32)

Rnds 3-9: sc in each st (32)

- Change to green.

Rnds 10-13: sc in each st (32)

Rnd 14: [invdec, sc 14] two times (30)

Rnds 15-18: sc in each st (30)

Rnd 19: [invdec, sc 8] three times (27)

- Change to medium gray. Stuff the body.

Rnd 20: sc in each st (27)

Extra stitches: sc as many as necessary to start the next rnd at the middle of the back (see page 38—Fig. A)

Rnd 21: sc, invdec, sc 9, inc, sc, inc, sc 9, invdec, sc (27)

Rnd 22: sc in each st (27)

Rnd 23: sc, invdec, sc 9, inc, sc, inc, sc 9, invdec, sc (27)

Rnds 24-25: sc in each st (27)

Rnd 26: sc 2, invdec, sc 9, inc, sc, inc, sc 9, invdec (27)

Rnds 27-30: sc in each st (27)

Rnd 31: [invdec, sc 7] three times (24)

Rnd 32: [sc 2, invdec] six times (18)

Rnd 33: [invdec, sc] six times (12)

- Stuff the head.

Rnd 34: invdec 6 (6)

- Fasten off and close the remaining hole.
- Embroider a belt with 2 strands of medium blue yarn and chain stitches.

FACE

- Start with dark gray yarn.

Rnd 1: make a magic ring and sc 6 (6)

Rnd 2: inc, sc, *change to ecru*, sc, inc, sc 2 (8)

Rnd 3: sc, *change to dark gray*, inc, sc, *change to ecru*, inc, sc, inc, sc, inc (12)

Rnd 4: [inc, sc 2] four times (16)

Rnd 5: [sc 3, inc] four times (20)

Rnd 6: sc, inc, sc, sl st 5, [inc, sc 3] three times (24)

Rnd 7: sc 3, sl st (4 st plus 20 unworked)

- Fasten off, leaving a long yarn end. Sew the face to the head, with the slip stitches at the bottom, 4 rnds above the green shirt. **(FIG. A—PAGE 50)**

- Embroider a mouth at the bottom of the dark gray nose patch using 4 strands of black floss. Mark the position of the eyes with pins (level with the center of the magic ring, 2 rnds from the edge of the face). With dark gray yarn embroider 2-3 slanted stitches to create the "tear marks." **(FIG. B—PAGE 50)**

- Glue the eyes in place. (If you don't have flat-backed eyes, cut off the shafts of the safety eyes with a wire cutter.) Once the glue has set, embroider eyelids with 2-3 horizontal dark gray stitches.

- Embroider hair with medium gray yarn. **(FIG. C—PAGE 50)**

ARMS (MAKE 2)

- Start with ecru yarn.

FIG. A

FIG. B

FIG. C

Rnd 1: make a magic ring and sc 6 (6)

Rnd 2: [inc, sc] three times (9)

Rnd 3: sc in each st (9)

Rnd 4: sc 4, *change to medium gray*, sc 5 (9)

Rnd 5: sc 4, inc, sc 3, inc (11)

Rnds 6-15: sc in each st (11)

Rnd 16: hdc 2, dc, hdc 2, sc 6 (11)

Rnds 17-20: sc in each st (11)

· Change to green.

Rnds 21-27: sc in each st (11)

· Sl st in next st and fasten off, leaving a long yarn end. Leave the ecru "claws" unstuffed, stuff the rest of the arms lightly. Sew the arms to body so that the elbows (created by the hdc and dc stitches) point outwards. **(FIG. D)**

FIG. D

· Flatten the ecru part from front and back. To suggest individual claws, embroider two lines with 2 strands of black floss. **(FIG. E)**

FIG. E

TIE

· Cut 2 pieces of dark blue and 2 of orange yarn, each about 12" long. Tie one orange strand around the middle of the other pieces. Pin the knot to something solid, and then arrange the yarn in 4 two-strand bunches, orange on the sides and blue in the middle **(FIG. F)**. Cross the bunch on the far left over the middle left. **(FIG. G—PAGE 52)** Cross the bunch on the far right over both middle right and middle left. **(FIG. H—PAGE 52)** Keep repeating to create a striped braid; pull the strands just so there's no slack but don't make the braid super tight. Tie a knot about 1.5" from the braid's tip (or as long as you want the tie to be), then undo the braid beyond the knot. Sew the tie to the neck using the yarn ends.

FIG. F

FIG. G

FIG. H

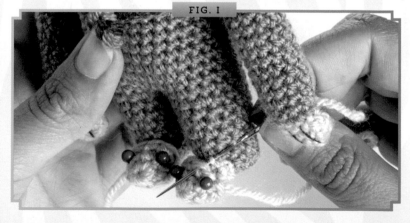

FIG. I

COLLAR (MAKE 2)

• Use green yarn.

Row 1: ch 8, sl st in the 2nd ch from hook, skip 2 ch, dc, hdc, sc, sl st (5)

• Fasten off, leaving a long yarn end.

• Sew the collar pieces to the neck beside the tie knot.

TOE CLAWS (MAKE 2)

• Use ecru yarn.

Rnd 1: make a magic ring and sc 6 (6)

Rnd 2: [sc 2, inc] two times (8)

Rnd 3: sc in each st (8)

• Sl st in next st and fasten off, leaving a long yarn end. Flatten the claws and sew them to the feet so that they point slightly inward. To suggest individual claws, embroider two lines on both top and bottom with 2 strands of black floss. **(FIG. J)**

8

DUKE WEASELTON

Also known as the Duke of Bootleg (by Nick anyway), Weaselton is a petty criminal whose only allegiance is to money. Besides peddling pirated movies, he will happily pick pockets or steal whatever he can turn around and sell, including night howler bulbs.

FINISHED SIZE: ABOUT 4.25"

MATERIALS

- Beige DK yarn
- Navy blue DK yarn
- Ecru DK yarn
- Red DK yarn
- Pair of black plastic safety eyes (6mm)
- White felt
- Black embroidery floss
- Stuffing
- D/3 crochet hook (3.25mm)
- Large needle

EYE PREPARATION

Use the template (page 75) to cut out the eye whites from the felt. Make a hole at the marked spot and push the eye stems though the felt. **(FIG. A)**

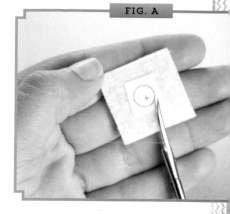

FIG. A

HEAD

• Use beige yarn.

Rnd 1: make a magic ring and sc 4 (4)

Rnd 2: inc, sc 3 (5)

Rnd 3: sc 4, inc (6)

Rnd 4: sc in each st (6)

Rnd 5: [sc, inc, sc] two times (8)

Rnd 6: [inc, sc] three times, sc 2 (11)

Rnd 7: sc, inc, sc 4, inc, sc 4 (13)

• Mark the 5th st of the rnd you just completed—this will show the top of the head. Stuff the muzzle.

Rnd 8: sc, [inc 2, sc 4] two times (17)

Rnd 9: sc 2, inc, sc, inc, sc 5, inc, sc, inc, sc 4 (21)

Rnd 10: sc in each st (21)

Rnd 11: sc 2, invdec, sc, invdec, sc 5, invdec, sc, invdec, sc 4 (17)

• Attach the eyes between rnds 7 and 8, about 3 st apart. **(FIG. B)** Remove the top-of-head marker.

Rnd 12: sc, invdec 2, sc, invdec, sc, invdec 2, sc 4 (12)

• Stuff the head.

Rnd 13: invdec 6 (6)

• Fasten off and close the remaining hole.

FIG. B

EARS (MAKE 2)

• Use beige yarn.

Rnd 1: make a magic ring and sc 6 (6)

Rnd 2: [inc, sc 2] two times (8)

Rnd 3: [inc, sc 3] two times (10)

• Fasten off, leaving a long end.

• Flatten the ear, then push the corners closer so that the ear base becomes

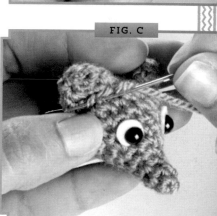

FIG. C

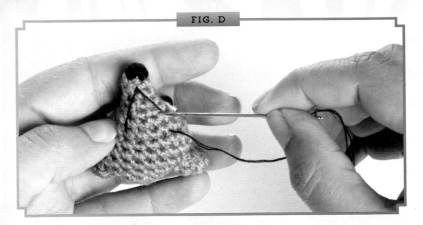

FIG. D

FIG. E

FIG. F

C shaped. Sew the ears to the head with the corners 3 rnds behind the eyes. **(FIG. C—PAGE 55)**

- Embroider the nose with 6 strands of black floss, then use 2 strands to create the mouth. **(FIG. D)**

LEGS (MAKE 2)

- Start with beige yarn.

Rnd 1: make a magic ring and sc 3, hdc 2, sc 3 (8)

Rnd 2: sc in each st (8)

Rnd 3: sc 2, invdec 2, sc 2 (6)

Rnd 4: sc in each st (6)

- Change to navy blue.

Rnd 5: sc in each st (6)

Rnd 6: inc, sc 5 (7)

- Sl st in next st and fasten off. Stuff the legs.

BODY

- Start with navy blue yarn.

Rnd 1: join the legs (see page 13) and sc around (12)

Rnd 2: [inc, sc 5] two times (14)

Rnds 3-4: sc in each st (14)

- Change to beige.

Rnds 5-6: sc in each st (14)

Rnd 7: [sc 5, invdec] two times (12)

- Change to ecru.

Rnds 8-11: sc in each st (12)

- Change to beige. Stuff the body.

Rnd 12: sc in each st (12)

Rnd 13: [invdec, sc 4] two times (10)

Rnds 14-16: sc in each st (10)

- Sl st in next st and fasten off, leaving a long yarn end. Stuff the neck.
- Embroider a red line on each side of the blue pants. **(FIG. E)**
- Sew the head to the body.

ARMS (MAKE 2)

- Use beige yarn.

Rnd 1: make a magic ring and sc 6 (6)

Rnds 2-9: sc in each st (6)

- Sl st in next st and fasten off, leaving a long yarn end.
- Sew the arms to the body, 2 rnds above the ecru top. With ecru yarn, make two long stitches circling each shoulder to create shoulder straps. **(FIG. F)**

TAIL

- Use beige yarn.

Rnd 1: make a magic ring and sc 5 (5)

Rnds 2-11: sc in each st (5)

- Sl st in next st and fasten off, leaving a long yarn end.
- Sew the tail to the body at rnd 3.

9

EMMITT OTTERTON

Emmitt Otterton is a florist who was the first to uncover the secret plot centered around the toxic night howler plants. Unfortunately, he himself was poisoned before he could tell anyone, and he ended up in the Cliffside Asylum with the other savage mammals.

FINISHED SIZE: ABOUT 4.5"

MATERIALS

- Brown DK yarn
- Beige DK yarn
- Purple DK yarn
- Khaki DK yarn
- Medium green DK yarn
- Light green DK yarn
- Dark green DK yarn

- Pair of black plastic safety eyes (6mm)
- White felt
- Black embroidery floss
- Stuffing
- D/3 crochet hook (3.25mm)
- Large needle

EYE PREPARATION

Cut a ½" square from felt and make a hole in the middle. Push the eye stem through and cut the felt off right around the eye. Repeat for the second eye. (see Fig. A, page 25)

HEAD

• Start with brown yarn.

Rnd 1: make a magic ring and sc 6 (6)

Rnd 2: inc 6 (12)

Rnd 3: [inc, sc] six times (18)

Rnd 4: sc 3, *to make the ear, ch 2, sl st in 2nd ch from hook*, sc 12, repeat **, sc 3 (18 sc plus ears) **(FIG. A)**

Rnd 5: sc 3, skip ear, sc 12, skip ear, sc 3 (18)

Rnd 6: [inc, sc] nine times (27)

Rnd 7: sc in each st (27)

Rnd 8: [sc, invdec] nine times (18)

Rnd 9: sc 2, invdec, sc 3, *change to beige*, sc, invdec, sc 2, *change to brown*, sc 2, invdec, sc 2 (15)

Rnd 10: sc 6, *change to beige*, sc 4, *change to brown*, sc 5 (15)

• Sl st to next st and fasten off.

• Insert the safety eyes between rnds 5 and 6, above the corners of the beige patch, but do not attach washers yet. **(FIG. B)** Stuff the head.

MUZZLE

• Use beige yarn.

Rnd 1: make a magic ring and sc 6 (6)

Rnd 2: [inc 2, sc] two times (10)

Rnd 3: sc 2, (sc, 2 hdc) in next st, sc 2, (2 hdc, sc) in next st, sc, sl st (12 st plus 2 unworked)

• Fasten off, leaving a long yarn end.

• Pinch together the piece at the hdc groups; this will turn the whole muzzle bean shaped. **(FIG. C)** Attach muzzle to the head just under the

FIG. A

FIG. B

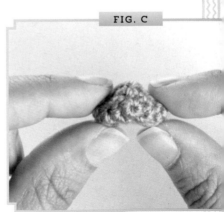

FIG. C

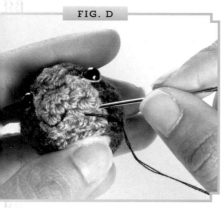

eyes, with the inward curve at the bottom.

- Remove stuffing from the head to attach the washers to the eyes, then stuff again.

NOSE

- Use purple yarn.

Row 1: ch 2, working in the 2nd ch from hook, make a puff st (see Fig. L, page 10), sl st in same ch, and fasten off, leaving a long yarn end.

- Sew the nose to the top of the muzzle.
- Embroider the mouth following the shape of the muzzle, using 2 strands of black floss. **(FIG. D)**

LEGS (MAKE 2)

- Start with brown yarn.

Rnd 1: make a magic ring and sc 5 (5)

Rnd 2: inc 5 (10)

Rnd 3: sc in each st (10)

Rnd 4: sc 3, invdec 2, sc 3 (8)

- Change to khaki.

Rnds 5-6: sc in each st (8)

Rnd 7: inc, sc 7 (9)

- Sl st in next st and fasten off. Stuff the legs.

BODY

- Start with khaki yarn.

Rnd 1: join the legs (see page 13) and sc around (16)

Rnd 2: [inc, sc 7] two times (18)

Rnd 3: sc in each st (18)

- Change to medium green.

Rnds 4-8: sc in each st (18)

Rnd 9: [invdec, sc 7] two times (16)

Rnds 10-12: sc in each st (16)

Rnd 13: invdec, sc 14 (15)

- Change to light green.

Rnd 14: sc in each st (15)

- Sl st in next st and fasten off, leaving a long yarn end. Stuff the body.

- Sew the head to the body. (Pause when there is only a small gap left and check if you need to add more stuffing to the neck.)

ARMS (MAKE 2)

- Start with brown yarn.

Rnd 1: make a magic ring and sc 6 (6)

Rnd 2: [inc, sc 2] two times (8)

Rnd 3: sc in each st (8)

- Change to light green.

Rnds 4–10: sc in each st (8)

- Change to medium green.

Rnd 11: sc 3, invdec, sc 3 (7)

- Sl st in next st and fasten off, leaving a long yarn end. Sew the arms to the body.

- With light green and chain stitches, embroider collar points to the neck. **(FIG. E)** Optionally, use dark green yarn to add decorative patterns to the vest: a straight line above the hem and zigzag lines over the chest. **(FIG. F)**

TAIL

- Use brown yarn.

Rnd 1: make a magic ring and sc 4 (4)

Rnd 2: [inc, sc] two times (6)

Rnd 3: sc in each st (6)

Rnd 4: [inc, sc 2] two times (8)

Rnds 5–12: sc in each st (8)

- Sl st in next st and fasten off, leaving a long yarn end. Sew the tail to the body at rnd 4.

10

MR. BIG

In Zootopia, anyone can be anything—and nothing proves this more than the tiny but ferocious shrew who is the most feared crime boss of Tundratown. Mr. Big is ruthless towards those who disrespect him, but he is very loyal to his friends and allies, and he dotes on his only daughter, Fru Fru.

FINISHED SIZE: ABOUT 3.5"

MATERIALS

- Gray DK yarn
- Pink DK yarn
- Black DK yarn
- White DK yarn
- Red DK yarn
- Black embroidery floss
- White felt
- Black felt

- 2mm green bead
- Gold sewing thread
- Fabric glue
- Stuffing
- D/3 crochet hook (3.25mm)
- Large needle
- Sewing or beading needle

HEAD

· Use gray yarn.

Rnd 1: make a magic ring and sc 6 (6)

Rnd 2: inc 6 (12)

Rnd 3: sc in each st (12)

Rnd 4: [inc, sc 2] four times (16)

Rnd 5: sc 3, *to make the ear, ch 3, sc in 3rd ch from hook*, sc 10, repeat **, sc 3 (16 sc plus ears) **(FIG. A)**

Rnd 6: inc 3, skip ear, inc 2, sc 6, inc 2, skip ear, inc 3 (26) **(FIG. B)**

Rnds 7-9: sc in each st (26)

Rnd 10: invdec 13 (13)

· Sl st in next st and fasten off. Stuff the head.

SNOUT

· Start with pink yarn.

Rnd 1: make a magic ring and sc 5 (5)

Rnd 2: sc in each st (5)

· Change to gray.

Rnds 3-4: sc in each st (5)

Rnd 5: inc, sc 4 (6)

Rnd 6: sc in each st (6)

Rnd 7: [inc, sc 2] two times (8)

· Sl st in next st and fasten off, leaving a long yarn end. The more bulging side of the head is the back side. Sew the snout to the flatter "face side" so that its top is level with the ears. **(FIG. C)**

HAIR

· Use black yarn.

Rnd 1: make a magic ring and sc 2, hdc, dc, hdc, sc 2 (7)

Rnd 2: sc, inc, sc, (hdc 2, ch 2, hdc 2) in next st, sc, inc, sc (14 st including chains)

· Sl st in next st and fasten off, leaving a long yarn end. Sew the hair to the head, covering the first 2 rnds on the front and reaching lower at the back. **(FIG. D)**

EYEBROWS (MAKE 2)

- Use black yarn.

Row 1: ch 6. Working in the back ridge of chains, hdc in 3rd ch from hook, sc, sl st 2 and fasten off, leaving a long yarn end (4)

- The eyebrows should be about one st apart above the snout, and slant downwards. **(FIG. E)** Sew them on only at the bottom and middle, but leave the top edge free.

- Embroider a mouth with 2 strands of black floss. **(FIG. F)**

LEGS (MAKE 2)

- Start with pink yarn.

Rnd 1: make a magic ring and sc 3, hdc 2, sc 3 (8)

- Change to white.

Rnd 2: sc 2, invdec 2, sc 2 (6)

- Change to black.

Rnd 3: sc in each st (6)

Rnd 4: [inc, sc 2] two times (8)

Rnd 5: [inc, sc 2] two times, inc, sc (11)

- Sl st in next st and fasten off.

BODY

- Use black yarn.

Rnd 1: join the legs (see page 13) and sc around (20)

Rnd 2: [inc, sc 9] two times (22)

Rnds 3–5: sc in each st (22)

Rnd 6: [invdec, sc 9] two times (20)

Rnd 7: sc in each st (20)

Rnd 8: [invdec, sc 8] two times (18)

Rnd 9: sc in each st (18)

Rnd 10: [invdec, sc 2] four times, invdec (13)

- Sl st in next st and fasten off, leaving a long yarn end.
- Stuff legs and body.
- Sew the head to the body. (Pause when there is only a small gap left and

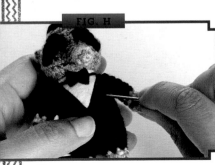

check if you need to add more stuffing to the neck.)

ARMS (MAKE 2)

· Start with pink yarn.

Rnd 1: make a magic ring and sc 6 (6)

Rnd 2: sc in each st (6)

· Change to white.

Rnd 3: sc in each st (6)

· Change to black.

Rnds 4-8: sc in each st (6)

· Sl st in next st and fasten off, leaving a long yarn end.

· Sew the arms to the body.

· Cut out the shirt triangle from white felt (template is on page 75). Push it towards the neck so that the two sides of the slit open up to make the collar. **(FIG. G)** Glue it to the body in this position.

· Cut out the tie from black felt. To turn the rectangle into a bow, tie a length of black yarn around the middle, then tie the bowtie around the neck.

· With red yarn, embroider a tiny star to the chest for his boutonniere. **(FIG. H)** Optionally, embroider jacket details with black yarn.

TAIL

· Use gray yarn.

Row 1: ch 9. Working in the back ridge of chains, sl st in 2nd ch from hook, sl st 7 (8)

· Fasten off, leaving a long yarn end.

· Sew the tail to the body.

· For his ring, sew the green bead to the right hand with gold thread.

KOSLOV

He is not a mammal of many words, but Koslov's devotion to Mr. Big is unquestionable. The biggest, scariest polar bear of the Tundratown mafia acts as personal bodyguard, preferred mode of transport, and occasionally even as viewing platform for his boss.

FINISHED SIZE: ABOUT 8"

MATERIALS

- Cream DK yarn
- Black DK yarn
- Pair of black plastic safety eyes (6mm)
- Black embroidery floss
- Size 20 crochet thread in gold
- Stuffing
- D/3 crochet hook (3.25mm)
- Steel crochet hook (1.5mm)
- Large needle

HEAD

• Use cream yarn and a D/3 hook.

Rnd 1: make a magic ring and sc 6 (6)

Rnd 2: inc 6 (12)

Rnd 3: [sc, inc] six times (18)

Rnd 4: [inc, sc 2] six times (24)

Rnd 5: [sc 7, inc] three times (27)

Rnds 6–9: sc in each st (27)

Rnd 10: [inc, sc 8] three times (30)

Rnds 11–14: sc in each st (30)

Rnd 15: [invdec, sc 3] six times (24)

Rnds 16–18: sc in each st (24)

• Sl st in next st and fasten off. Attach safety eyes between rnds 7 and 8, about 5 st apart. Stuff the head.

MUZZLE

• Use cream yarn and a D/3 hook.

Rnd 1: make a magic ring and sc 6 (6)

Rnd 2: inc 6 (12)

Rnd 3: [inc, sc 3] three times (15)

Rnd 4: sc in each st (15)

Rnd 5: [inc, sc 4] three times (18)

Rnds 6–7: sc in each st (18)

• Sl st in next st and fasten off, leaving a long yarn end.

• Stuff the muzzle and sew it to the head so that the highest point is between the eyes.

• Embroider the nose with black yarn, then make a slanted stitch above each eye to create the eyebrows. Embroider the mouth with 3 strands of black floss. **(Figs. A & B)**

EARS (MAKE 2)

• Use cream yarn and a D/3 hook.

Rnd 1: make a magic ring and sc 5 (5)

Rnd 2: inc 5 (10)

Rnds 3–4: sc in each st (10)

• Sl st in next st and fasten off, leaving a long yarn end.

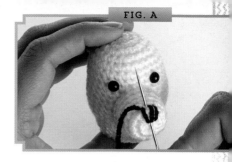

FIG. A

FIG. B

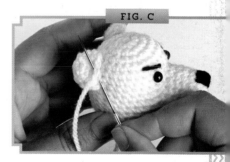

FIG. C

FIG. D

FIG. E

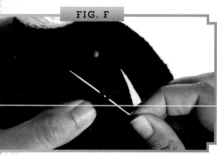

FIG. F

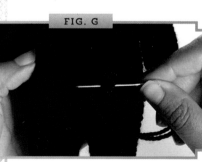

FIG. G

FIG. H

- Flatten the ears and sew them to the sides of the head; the lower corner should be level with the bottom of the eyes. **(FIG. C—PAGE 67)**

LEGS (MAKE 2)

- Start with cream yarn and a D/3 hook.

Rnd 1: make a magic ring and sc 6 (6)

Rnd 2: inc 6 (12)

Rnd 3: [inc, sc] six times (18)

Rnds 4–5: sc in each st (18)

Rnd 6: sc 5, [invdec, sc] three times, sc 4 (15)

- Change to black.

Rnds 7–8: sc in each st (15)

Rnd 9: [sc 4, inc] three times (18)

Rnds 10–11: sc in each st (18)

Rnd 12: [sc 8, inc] two times (20)

Rnds 13–14: sc in each st (20)

- Sl st in next st and fasten off. Stuff the legs.

BODY

- Use black yarn and a D/3 hook.

Rnd 1: join the legs (see page 13) and sc around (38)

Rnd 2: [inc, sc 8] four times, sc 2 (42)

Rnd 3: sc in each st (42)

Rnd 4: sc 2, [inc, sc 9] four times (46)

Rnds 5–12: sc in each st (46)

Rnd 13: [invdec, sc 21] two times (44)

Rnds 14–15: sc in each st (44)

Rnd 16: [invdec, sc 20] (42)

Rnds 17–18: sc in each st (42)

Rnd 19: [sc 6, invdec, sc 6] three times (39)

Rnds 20–21: sc in each st (39)

Rnd 22: [invdec, sc 11] three times (36)

Rnds 23–24: sc in each st (36)

Rnd 25: [invdec, sc 7] four times (32)

Rnd 26: sc in each st (32)

Rnd 27: [sc 3, invdec, sc 3] four times (28)

Rnd 28: sc in each st (28)

Rnd 29: [invdec, sc 5] four times (24)

Rnd 30: sl st, ch 3, working in FLO for the rest of the round, dc in the same st as the sl st, dc 23 (24 dc)

- Sl st in the top of the ch 3, fasten off, and weave in the end.
- The top rnd will become the turtleneck. Flip it down to reveal the unworked loops left by the FLO stitches; you will sew the head to these loops only. Stuff the body, then sew the head to the neck with black yarn. **(FIG. D—PAGE 67)** Fold the turtleneck back up.

ARMS (MAKE 2)

- Start with cream yarn and a D/3 hook.

Rnd 1: make a magic ring and sc 6 (6)

Rnd 2: inc 6 (12)

Rnd 3: [inc, sc 3] three times (15)

Rnds 4–6: sc in each st (15)

- Change to black.

Rnds 7–25: sc in each st (15)

Rnd 26: [invdec, sc 3] three times (12)

- Sl st in next st and fasten off, leaving a long yarn end.
- Stuff the arms lightly and sew them to the body.

JACKET EDGING

- Use black yarn and a D/3 hook.

Row 1: ch 77. Sc in the 2nd ch from hook, dc 6, hdc 2, sc 10, (sc, ch 2, sc) in next ch, sc 36, (sc, ch 2, sc) in next ch, sc 10, hdc 2, dc 6, sc. **(FIG. E)** Sl st in the same st as the last sc and fasten off, leaving a long yarn end.

- The "sc 36" part should go around the body roughly at rnd 6, with the two ends horizontally up on the front. Pin the piece to the body and sew the chain side to the body, leaving the other edge free. **(FIG. F)**
- Use 2 strands of black yarn and chain

stitches to embroider a belt between the jacket edgings, at rnd 8. **(FIG. G)**

JEWELRY

- Use gold thread and steel crochet hook.

Rnd 1: make a magic ring and hdc 9. Sl st into the top of the first hdc, then ch until the piece measures 8" long (about 75 ch) and fasten off.

- Sew the medallion to the body using the end from the magic ring. Then thread the crocheted chain into a large needle and use it as a single strand to embroider the rest of the necklace. **(FIG. H)**

GAZELLE

Gazelle is the favorite pop star of Zootopia, but she is admired for more than just a beautiful voice or pretty face: she is a devoted mammal rights activist, using her fame to promote acceptance and equality among all animals of her beloved city.

FINISHED SIZE: ABOUT 7"

MATERIALS

- Cream DK yarn
- Tan DK yarn
- Brown DK yarn
- Beige DK yarn
- Red DK yarn (preferably sparkly red)
- Pair of black plastic safety eyes (6mm)
- Pink embroidery floss
- Black embroidery floss
- Lilac embroidery floss
- Sewing thread (or embroidery floss) in cream
- Stuffing
- D/3 crochet hook (3.25mm)
- Large needle
- Sewing or embroidery needle (optional)

HEAD

- Start with cream yarn.

Rnd 1: make a magic ring and sc 6 (6)

Rnd 2: inc, sc, *change to tan*, inc, *change to cream*, sc, inc, sc (9)

Rnd 3: sc 3, *change to tan*, sc 2, *change to cream*, sc 4 (9)

- Change to tan.

Rnd 4: [inc, sc 2] three times (12)

Rnd 5: sc in each st (12)

Rnd 6: sc 5, inc, sc 2, inc, sc 3 (14)

Rnd 7: sc 6, inc, sc 2, inc, sc 4 (16)

Rnds 8–10: sc in each st (16)

- Attach safety eyes between rnds 6 and 7, about 6 st apart (the tan st in rnd 2 and 3 show the top side of the head). **(FIG. A)**

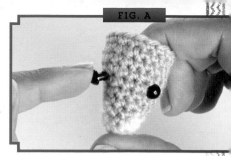

FIG. A

Rnd 11: [invdec, sc 2] four times (12)

- Stuff the head.

Rnd 12: invdec 6 (6)

- Fasten off and close the remaining hole.

- With cream yarn, embroider two chain stitch lines from the nose to behind the eyes. **(FIG. B)** Use a single strand of pink floss to outline the nose and mouth, then add a few more stitches to the nose for thicker lines. **(FIG. C)** With 3 strands of black floss, embroider a slanted line backwards from each eye, then make several stitches above the black line with three strands of lilac floss. **(FIG. D)** (For these fine details, a small embroidery or sewing needle might be more suitable than the large yarn needle.)

FIG. B

FIG. C

EARS (MAKE 2)

- Use tan yarn.

Row 1: ch 6. Working in the back ridge of chains sc in 2nd ch from hook, hdc 3, sc (5)

- Fasten off, leaving a long yarn end, and sew the ears to the head; they should be level with the eyes and 3 rnds behind them. **(FIG. E—PAGE 72)**

FIG. D

FIG. E

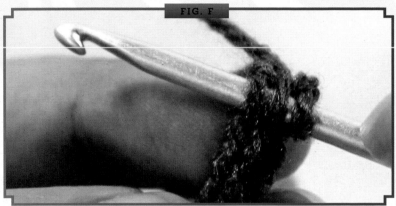

FIG. F

FIG. G

HORNS (MAKE 2)

• Use brown yarn.

Row 1: ch 9. Working in the back ridge of chains, sl st in 2nd ch from hook, sl st 7 (8)

Row 2: ch 1, turn. Inserting your hook through the closest loops of the sl st and the foundation ch, sl st 8 (8) **(FIG. F)**

• Fasten off, leaving a long yarn end. Weave in the other ends and sew the horns to the top of the head at rnd 10.

LEGS (MAKE 2)

• Start with beige yarn.

Rnd 1: make a magic ring and sc 3, hdc 2, sc 3 (8)

Rnd 2: working in BLO this round, sc in each st (8)

• Change to red.

Rnd 3: sc 2, invdec 2, sc 2 (6)

Rnds 4-5: sc in each st (6)

Rnd 6: inc, sc 5 (7)

Rnds 7-9: sc in each st (7)

• Change to tan.

Rnd 10: inc, sc 6 (8)

Rnds 11-13: sc in each st (8)

Rnd 14: [inc, sc 3] two times (10)

Rnds 15-16: sc in each st (10)

• Sl st in next st and fasten off. Stuff the legs.

BODY

• Start with tan yarn.

Rnd 1: join the legs (see page 13) and sc around (18)

Rnd 2: [inc, sc 8] two times (20)

Rnds 3-4: sc in each st (20)

Rnd 5: [sc 4, invdec, sc 4] two times (18)

Rnd 6: [invdec, sc 7] two times (16)

Rnd 7: sc in each st (16)

• Change to red.

Rnd 8: [sc 3, invdec, sc 3] two times (14)

FIG. H

BACK THIRD OF NECK

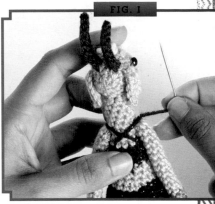

FIG. I

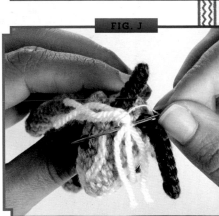

FIG. J

Rnds 9–10: sc in each st (14)

• Mark the stitch that is in the front middle.

Rnd 11: sc until the marker, *change to tan*, remove marker and sc, *change to red*, sc to the remaining st (14) **(FIG. G—PAGE 72)**

• Change to tan. Stuff the body.

Rnd 12: sc in each st (14)

Rnd 13: sc 2, [invdec, sc] four times (10)

Rnds 14–15: sc in each st (10)

Rnd 16: invdec, sc 8 (9)

Rnds 17–18: sc in each st (9)

Rnd 19: find the 3 st that make the back third of the neck. **(FIG. H—PAGE 73)** If necessary, sc until you reach the first of these stitches, hdc 3, sc, sl st (unfinished round)

• Fasten off, leaving a long yarn end. Stuff the neck.

SKIRT

• Use red yarn.

Rnd 1: ch 18. Sc in the first ch to join in a circle (take care not to twist the chain). Sc 7, inc, sc 8, inc (20)

• Work the rest of the skirt **in BLO**.

Rnd 2: [sc 4, inc, sc 5] two times (22)

Rnd 3: [inc, sc 10] two times (24)

Rnds 4–6: sc in each st (24)

• Sl st in next st and fasten off, weave in yarn ends. Sew the skirt to the waist with red yarn, 3 rnds below the top.

• Sew the head to the body.

ARMS (MAKE 2)

• Use beige yarn.

Rnd 1: make a magic ring and sc 6 (6)

Rnd 2: working in BLO this rnd, sc in each st (6)

• Change to tan.

Rnds 3–14: sc in each st (6)

• Fasten off, leaving a long yarn end. Sew the arms to the body.

• Embroider shoulder straps with red yarn. **(FIG. I—PAGE 73)**

TAIL

• Use tan yarn.

Rnd 1: make a magic ring and sc 6 (6)

Rnds 2–3: sc in each st (6)

Rnd 4: invdec, sc 4 (5)

Rnd 5: sc in each st (5)

• Fasten off, leaving a long yarn end, and sew the tail to the top of the skirt.

• For her hairstyle, cut three 3" pieces of cream yarn. Tie them together at the middle with cream thread (or a strand of floss), fold the bunch in half and sew it to the head, just in front of the horns. **(FIG. J—PAGE 73)** Separate the plies of the yarn, trim them to the right length, then if necessary use hair mousse to style them.

Templates

DUKE TEMPLATE

BELLWETHER TEMPLATE

LIONHEART TEMPLATE

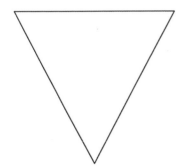

MR. BIG TEMPLATE

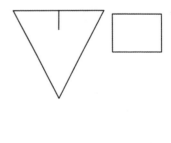

About the Author

Kati Gálusz discovered the world of amigurumi when she wanted to make a unique gift for a toy-collector friend. What started as a quick fling has grown into the love of a lifetime, allowing her to combine her need for creativity with her main interests: animals, great books, and movies. After lavishing her creations on her long-suffering family and friends, she started to sell them on Etsy (lunascrafts.etsy.com) and share her crochet patterns on Ravelry (http://www.ravelry.com/designers/kati-galusz). When she is not crocheting, she can be usually found with a book in her hand, surrounded by her dogs, in her home near Budapest, Hungary.

Acknowledgments

A big thank-you to Dana for the opportunity to be part of this project, and to all the people at becker&mayer! whose talent contributed to this book. And many thanks to my family, who encouraged my yarn obsession from the very beginning.